What's Different About Trevor?

A Seven Lions Story

To: Anna
We hope you enjoy our book

Samantha

liv

By Michael, Olivia & Samantha Mortlock

For Arthur & Greta
who enjoyed our stories so much,
they inspired us to write them down

Text and illustrations copyright © 2017
Michael, Olivia & Samantha Mortlock

ISBN: 978-981-11-4348-9

Once upon a time there were seven lions.
Their names were...

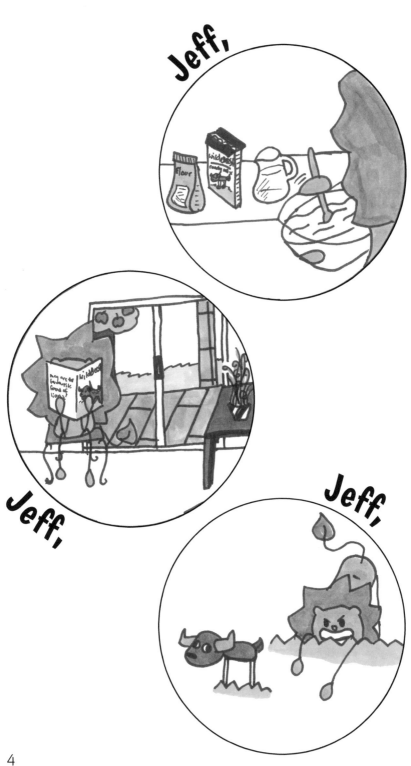

These lions didn't live wild and free on the African savannah like other lions and they didn't live caged in a city zoo either.

These lions lived, much like you
and me, in a house in the suburbs
on the edge of town.

Being lions, they loved wildebeest!

Wildebeest steaks, wildebeest sausages, wildebeest crisps - they even ate wildebeest flavoured popcorn whilst watching their favourite TV shows on the wildebeest channel.

One rainy day, the lions were all lounging about at home watching, as usual, the wildebeest channel. A group of wildebeest had just managed to avoid getting eaten and the lions all booed the TV, except for Trevor, who had his snout stuck in a bag of wildebeest crisps.

One of the Jeffs noticed this and said, *"you know, there is something different about you Trevor."* All the other Jeffs stopped what they were doing, crowded around Trevor, pointed at him and chorused, *"there is something different about you Trevor."*

Trevor jumped up from the sofa and shouted, *"WHAT, WHAT IS DIFFERENT?"* and started chasing his tail in circles.

The Jeffs decided to take a more scientific
approach to the problem and made a list
of things to check.

→ Height
→ weight

→ no. whiskers
→ tail length
pantone colour chart

They started by measuring Trevor's height.
There was no difference...

They checked his weight. There was
no difference...

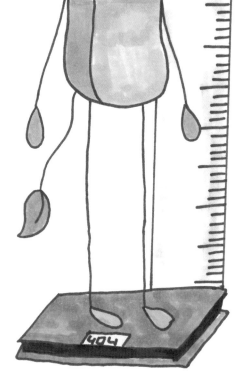

They counted his whiskers, but he had eight
like all the others...

1...2...7...4...23...

5 6 7 8

1 2 3 4

75.5cm

They measured
the length of his
tail. It was also
the same length
as the Jeffs.

They even went so far as to check the colour of his fur using a pantone colour chart...

but this did not help at all.

"You know," said Trevor after a lot of head scratching. *"It could be that I have a different name to the rest of you guys."*

The Jeffs all looked at each other slightly puzzled, then one of them replied, *"don't be silly Trevor, that is not it!"*

The Jeffs got into a huddle to decide on their next steps and lots of whispering ensued.

Meanwhile Trevor took the opportunity to finish off all the wildebeest crisps and popcorn.

At last the Jeffs finished brainstorming and they turned around to tell Trevor their latest clever scheme to find out why he was different. When they discovered that Trevor had eaten all of their snacks they all roared together.

"Trevor, you are sooo different!"

Which shook the house and made the neighbours cower in fright.

"*Prove it,*" countered Trevor, whilst licking wildebeest flavouring off his whiskers.

"*Ah ha,*" said one of the Jeffs, "*we will. We will take you to the doctor and he will tell us what is different about you.*" All the Jeffs looked immensely proud of this revelation and gave each other high fives to celebrate.

Jeff called a taxi to take them to the doctor's office and Trevor went out to the front of the house to wait for the taxi to arrive.

Ten minutes later, Trevor came back inside to ask Jeff to call another taxi.

"*What happened to the first taxi?*" asked Jeff.

"*Ummm, I might have accidentally eaten the driver,*" replied Trevor. Jeff groaned in frustration and called another taxi.

While Trevor was moving the empty taxi into their garage, Jeff went out to wait for the new taxi.

growl

Five minutes later after Trevor had finished hiding the first taxi, Jeff came back inside looking sheepish and asked Jeff to call yet another taxi.

"*Oh, not you too,*" growled Jeff as he reached for the phone to call another taxi. "*This time we will all wait together and NO EATING the drivers.*"

Eventually they arrived at the doctor's office and after eating their taxi driver, they trooped into the waiting area.

The receptionist, who was a severe looking elderly lady, looked very unimpressed with a large group of lions invading her waiting room.

When Jeff asked politely to see the doctor, she checked her appointment book and replied, *"the doctors schedule is full and you cannot see him if you do not have an appointment."* She sat back in her chair looking satisfied with herself.

25

Jeff looked around at the waiting room full of sick people and flicked his ears at the rest of the lions.

Two minutes later the waiting room was empty, except for a few scraps of clothes and two of the Jeffs let out very loud burps. *"We should do this more often,"* commented one of the Jeffs.

Jeff turned back to the now horrified looking receptionist and asked, *"is it possible to see the doctor now?"*

"*I am sorry,*" trembled the receptionist, "*the doctor only sees human patients. Since you are lions you will need to go to a vet.*"

Jeff roared angrily and quickly ate the receptionist.

"*So, where do we find a vet?*" asked Jeff.

"*I am sure the receptionist could have told us,*" joked Trevor, causing all the Jeffs to roar with laughter and the doctor to pee his pants in the other room.

Out on the street, the door to the doctors office suddenly flew open and seven lions came bursting out onto the street scaring most of the passers-by and causing a cyclist to crash into a park bench.

Jeff bounded up to the nearest pedestrian and loudly demanded, *"where is the nearest vet?"* The man promptly fainted with fright before he could answer causing Jeff to roar in frustration, further scaring the public.

Trevor rolled his eyes at Jeff and said, *"Jeff – you need to be more subtle than that if you want to get answers."* He crouched down on the pavement and slowly crept towards a group of women who were sitting on a park bench.

When he was only a couple of metres away, he pounced over the park bench and landed right on top of a rather posh looking lady wearing a fancy hat.

"*Where is the vet,*" he roared directly in her face. To her credit, the posh lady didn't faint and managed to point down the street. "*That way,*" she said, "*go straight for two blocks then turn left and the vet is just there.*"

"See," said Trevor with a smug grin, *"told you,"* and he bounded off down the street in the wrong direction.

"TREEEEVVVOORRR!!!!"
cried all the Jeffs together,
"YOU'RE GOING THE WRONG WAY!!!"

A rather sheepish looking Trevor slunk back to the group of lions and they all headed off together in the right direction.

Jeff shook his head and looked sideways at Trevor, *"definitely something different about that one,"* he muttered under his breath.

A short while later, the lions arrived at the vet's office and Jeff bounded through the door first. The other lions all tried to follow and got jammed in the doorway. After a lot of pushing and shoving, they managed to squeeze themselves through the door and into the front office only to discover that...

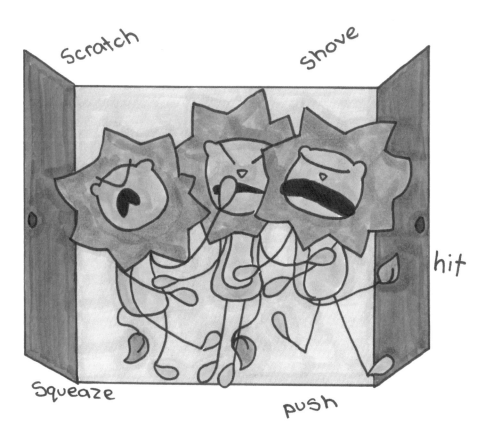

Jeff had already eaten the receptionist and the vet on duty.

AAAAAAAAGHH!

"*It was an accident,*" claimed Jeff as the other lions all looked at him accusingly. "*I tripped and they just kind of fell into my mouth.*" The lions looked at each other confused for a second, then roared with laughter.

"*Well,*" said Trevor, "*I guess that's that then,*" and they all trooped out of the vet's office and down the hill to the taxi stand.

Halfway down the hill, Jeff started bouncing up and down and pointing going, "*ooh ooh ooh.*" They followed his pointed paw and noticed that there was another vet clinic. In fact, there were two vet clinics, right next to each other.

"*Looks like it's our lucky day lads,*" called Jeff as he bounded toward the two vet clinics.

"*Make sure you don't trip again,*" called Trevor trying to catch up.

They leaped into the front office and as usual demanded to see the vet immediately.

Luckily for them, all the other patients had run away and hid as soon as they came in, so they could see the vet straight away.

In the clinic, the vet cowered in a corner
while the Jeffs stood over him and shouted,
"why is he different," pointing at Trevor.
"Why? Why? Why?"

After much roaring and gnashing of teeth, the vet finally understood what they wanted and started taking observations.

As before, he measured Trevor's height and weight.

Counted all his toes, whiskers and spots...

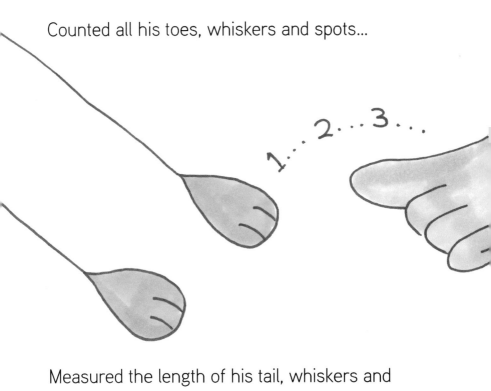

Measured the length of his tail, whiskers and toenails...

43

He even took his temperature!

"Can we hurry this along" asked Jeff checking his watch.

"It is nearly time for *"Wheel-debeest of Fortune."*

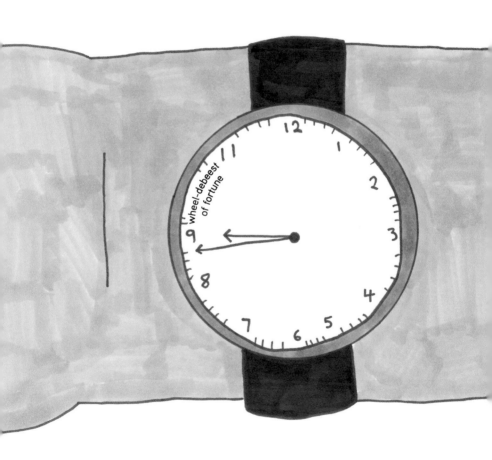

The vet could not find any differences at all,
so he asked them all to fill out a survey on diet,
likes/dislikes and habits.

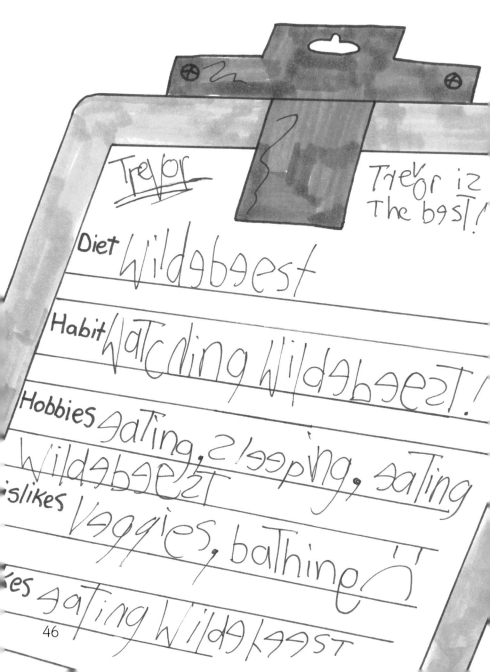

Trevor

Trevor iz
The best!

Diet Wildabeest

Habit Watching Wildabeezt!

Hobbies eating, sleeping, eating
Wildabeezt

slikes Veggies, bathing IT

es eating Wildabeest

After a quick read through of the surveys,
the vet finally noticed something.

"Aha," he cried standing up, *"I have it."*
The lions all crowded around anxious
to hear what the vet had found.

He pointed a quivering finger at Trevor
and announced in a confident voice,

"he has a different name
to the rest of you."

There was silence for nearly ten seconds
before Jeff spoke up.

"No, that is not it. You are a terrible vet,"
and he quickly scoffed him down.

Somewhat dejected, the lions all trooped
next door to the other vet.

They went through the entire
process all over again - measuring,
counting, questioning - although
Trevor's growl when the vet got out
his thermometer, convinced him to
skip that test.

After all the tests, the vet sat down and pondered the results.

"What is the answer Doc?" asked Jeff adding, *"by the way, we ate the last vet who suggested it is Trevor's name."*

The vet quickly scratched that answer off his pad and went back to thinking. After a few minutes he came up with an idea.

"Just one more test to do," he told the lions.

He got out his little rubber hammer used for testing reflexes and secretly dipped it in his black ink bottle.

Getting Trevor to sit on his exam bed, he lightly tapped his knee with the hammer a few times, leaving a black smudge of ink.

As expected, Trevor's leg jumped out when tapped and the vet told the Jeffs that this was completely normal and not different at all.

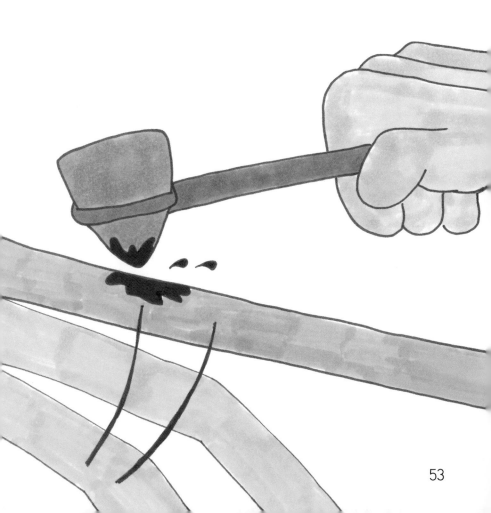

As the doctor was heading back to his desk Jeff suddenly started jumping and pointing at Trevor's knee.

"Hey Hey," he cried, "Trevor has an extra spot.... that must be what is different about him."

The Jeffs all cheered and gave each other high fives for finally figuring out what was different about Trevor.

Trevor himself kept looking at his knee in confusion, wondering why he had never noticed that spot before.

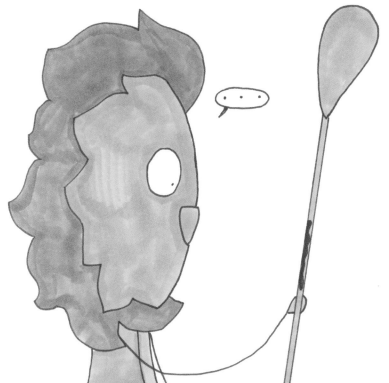

They all trooped out to the front office and started to head out onto the street when the vet called them back and presented them with the vet bill.

S $200
In the investigation of TREVOR we found an extra spot located on TREVORS KNEE,

Trevor stared at the bit of paper, then at the vet, then back at the paper again, then he ate it and the vet.

The lions then all scampered out into the street, laughing and roaring.

Fifteen minutes later, a taxi careened around the corner and into the street where the lions lived, narrowly missed a parked car and then crashed into a lampost.

The lions all piled out of the taxi and one of the Jeffs smacked another on the shoulder.

"That's why we don't eat taxi drivers while they are driving stupid," he berated him.

"Oh right," said Jeff, *"now I remember."*

The lions all headed inside the house where they settled themselves in front of the TV on couches, chairs and beanbags and with all their favourite wildebeest snacks. And there they stayed until their next big adventure.

THE END!!

About the Authors

The Seven Lion Stories are a family creation by
Michael, Olivia & **Samantha Mortlock**. They were
born on long train journeys around Japan on a family
holiday. Michael enjoys making up silly stories, Olivia
brought the stories to life with her wonderful drawings,
and Samantha provided the excellent colouring.

Acknowledgements

Our first thanks has to go to **Katie Mortlock** for not
only putting up with all our silliness, but helping with
the scanning, typing and admin involved in getting our
book ready to publish.

Our very special thanks to **Siska Laurentia** for her
wonderful graphic design skills. Without her, we would
still be wondering how to combine words and images.